GAME ON!

BATTLE OF THE BOTS

By Kevin Miller

www.bakkenbooks.com

Battle of the Bots by Kevin Miller
Copyright © 2024 Bakken Books

All rights reserved. This book is protected under the copyright laws of the United States of America. This book may not be copied or reprinted for commercial gain or profit. This book is a work of fiction. The Game On series is a work of fiction. Names, characters, businesses, places, events, incidents, and other locales are either the products of the author's imagination or used in a fictitious manner. Any resemblance to actual persons, living or dead, or actual events is purely coincidental.

ISBN: 978-1-963915-06-8
Published by Bakken Books
For Worldwide Distribution
Printed in the USA

www.bakkenbooks.com

Other Bakken Books Stories

Camping books for kids

Mystery books for kids

Hunting books for kids

Fishing books for kids

www.bakkenbooks.com

Math adventures for kids

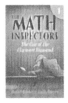  

History adventures for kids

Space adventures for kids

Humorous adventures for kids

- 1 -

"Yikes! Is that a rat?" I shrieked, not at all liking the high-pitched sound of my voice. Already a couple of years into puberty, I thought the days of cracks and croaks were well behind me. Then again, that was *before* I allowed Lucas to talk me and the rest of the Stream Team into accompanying him to the local landfill.

Why were we there? It all came down to a perennial debate among *Rumble Royale* players—console vs. PC. Having done his research, Lucas was convinced there really was no debate. While playing on a console like an Xbox, PlayStation, or

KEVIN MILLER

Nintendo Switch offered players a few advantages, such as aim assist, that function only worked well at certain ranges. Plus, console players were disadvantaged in nearly every other way, from building to editing to swapping weapons. And even with aim assist, there was no way a thumb on a joystick could match the precision of a mouse.

As proof of his theory, Lucas pointed out that not a single Rumble Royale Championship Series (RRCS) winner had earned their victory on a console. So, if we were to have any hope of winning a Rumble Royale Cash Cup, never mind the grand prize of $3 million, we really only had one choice: all of us had to play on a PC.

Having tried both options, I couldn't have agreed more—not that I was going to give Lucas the satisfaction of knowing that—but there was one teensy, weensy problem. Only a couple of us owned PCs, me being one of them.

Lucas was one of the squad members who didn't own a PC, nor could he afford one, hence our trip to the dump. That's because the landfill wasn't just a place where people took their garbage. It was also where they dropped off items to be recycled, such as computers. On a recent trip there with his dad, Lucas had noticed several pallets stacked high with discarded PCs, monitors, and other components, so he was confident that, if given a chance to dig through that pile, he'd be able to scrounge up enough parts to cobble together his own Frankencomputer.

Even though the stuff was at the dump, it wasn't like we could just waltz in and take it. Despite being labeled as trash, those computers contained all sorts of rare metals and other components that could be recycled and sold. So, before we could begin digging through it, we had to get permission from the people in charge.

As you can imagine, when all four of us rolled up to the landfill's entrance on our bikes, the attendant in the booth didn't exactly greet us with open arms. Instead, she met us with an arched eyebrow and a confused frown.

"Can I help you?" she asked, her eyes glancing around as if to see if we had arrived with any garbage to drop off like everyone else in line, all of whom were in vehicles rather than on bicycles.

"Yes, we're looking for some computer parts," Lucas said, having agreed to act as our spokesperson, seeing as going to the landfill was his idea.

"This isn't Best Buy," the attendant pointed out with a forced smile, "in case you haven't noticed."

"We realize that," Lucas replied, unfazed by her sarcasm. "We're looking for *used* computer parts, and it appears you have plenty of them right over there." He pointed to the pallets he had seen earlier. The attendant craned her neck to look at them, then turned back to us.

"What makes you think you can have them? Besides, we can't let a bunch of kids go roaming around the dump on their own. It isn't safe. So, if you'd kindly turn your bikes around and—"

"We're hardly kids, ma'am," Lucas said. "We're teenagers."

The attendant snorted in amusement. "Even worse."

"And we'll be sure to stay out of people's way," Lucas continued. "Darian here is the head of our school's mindfulness club, which makes him very grounded and trustworthy. Isn't that right, Darian?"

BATTLE OF THE BOTS

Darian waved to the attendant and smiled as Lucas pointed him out.

"And Shu is a Chinese exchange student," Lucas added. "Have you ever observed how respectful Chinese people are to their elders?"

To emphasize his point, Shu pressed the palms of her hands together and bowed to the woman, nearly folding her body in half.

"As for Wyatt, well . . ." Lucas held his index finger to his chin as he gave me a once-over, obviously struggling to think of something positive to say.

"I'm very responsible, ma'am," I said. "My parents ask me to babysit my little sister all the time." Lucas frowned at my weak attempt to justify myself, but hey, it was the best I could come up with on short notice.

"What about you, Shaq?" the attendant asked, a reference to Lucas's tall, gangly frame. "Why should I let *you* in?"

Lucas paused to assess the woman before offering a reply. "Have you ever had a dream, ma'am?"

I know what you're thinking: considering she was well past middle age and working as an attendant at a landfill, probably not. But then again . . .

"Yes," she replied, smiling. "When I was a little girl, I wanted to be a ballerina. I know, ridiculous, right?" she added, gesturing to her rather rotund body.

"What happened?" Lucas asked. "That is, how did you go from that dream to working in a place like . . . this?"

I was worried she would be offended by his question, but instead the woman chuckled to herself. "That's a long story, kid."

"I'll bet it's interesting," Lucas replied. "I'd love to hear it."

I couldn't help but stare at him in amazement. In the short time I'd known Lucas, he had displayed an uncanny ability to drive people away from him, not win them over. But judging from the look on the woman's face, I could tell his apparent interest in her life had cut straight through to her heart.

"What did you say you needed those computer parts for again?"

"I have my own dream, ma'am," Lucas replied. "We all do," he added, gesturing to the rest of us. "And those computer parts are the key."

BATTLE OF THE BOTS

Someone in the lineup honked their horn, but the woman waved a dismissive hand toward them, indicating they would have to wait. Scanning our faces again, she took a huge breath and then puffed out her cheeks, letting the air out through her mouth. "You're lucky my supervisor went home early today," she said. "I'll tell you what. You have fifteen minutes to dig through those pallets and take whatever you can carry. But I'm warning you: make a mess, and you're leaving here empty-handed. Got it?"

"Yes, ma'am," Lucas said, already pedaling away from the booth. "Thank you!"

"Yes, thank you!" I added. Shu bowed again, and Darian also voiced his gratitude as we set off after Lucas.

And that's how we found ourselves at the landfill, my fear of being bitten by a rabid rat only the beginning of our challenges.

- 2 -

"I don't see how we're going to find enough usable components here to build even one PC, never mind two," I said once we were a few minutes into our search. The second PC was for Shu, who hadn't brought one over from China. Thankfully, Darian already had a computer, although as I would soon learn, it wasn't exactly ideal for our purposes. "This stuff has all been sitting out in the rain," I continued. "Some of these cases even have rust on them."

"Dig deeper into the pile," Lucas replied as he did exactly that. "The ones lower down should be more protected, especially with all this shrink wrap around the pallet. Besides, just because the cases are rusty doesn't mean the insides are. And remember, we don't need the entire computer to work—just some of the parts."

"But how can we tell which parts still work and which don't?" Darian asked. He and Shu stood and watched as Lucas and I combed through the goods, the two of us being the only members of the group who had any idea what we were looking for.

"We can't," Lucas said as he plunked a large PC tower on top of the pile and examined the various inputs on the back. "Not until we plug it in. But trust me: we take enough of them, and we'll be able to make something work."

"You're going to take more than one computer?" Darian asked. "But how are we going to get them all home?"

Lucas paused his search and looked at our bikes as if suddenly remembering how we had arrived at the landfill. Our original plan had been to find components in various computers that looked promising. Then we would remove them and carry them home in our backpacks, which each of us had brought for that purpose. But with only fifteen minutes to search, there was barely time to find any promising candidates, never mind disassemble them.

"Why don't I text my dad?" I suggested, pulling out my cell phone.

"Can he get here in less than fifteen minutes?" Darian asked, checking his watch.

"I'm not sure," I replied, having no idea where my dad was or if he was even available.

"Just call him," Lucas said, hopping on his bike and heading back toward the booth. "I'll see if I can get us an extension."

Sure enough, Lucas was able to work his charm on the attendant once again. By the time he was done with her, I'm sure she would have allowed us to back up a dump truck and take anything we wanted. Instead, about fifteen minutes later, my dad showed up with our minivan, and we loaded our finds into the back.

"Are you sure you can make something functional out of all this junk?" Darian asked as my dad closed the van's rear door.

BATTLE OF THE BOTS

"Definitely," Lucas replied, the picture of confidence.

"And where exactly do you plan to do that?" Dad inquired.

"Uh, that reminds me," I said, shooting a glance at Lucas, who nodded for me to proceed. "I was wondering if I could ask you for another favor..."

That favor was permission to use our garage as a temporary computer workshop. My parents usually parked their vehicles there, but Dad agreed to park outside for the time being.

When I asked Lucas why we couldn't haul the salvaged computers to his place and do the work there, seeing as he was heading up the project, he mumbled something that I didn't quite understand. Even so, the meaning was clear: there was no way that was going to happen. In fact, whenever anything connected to Lucas's home life came up, he tended to give the same sort of vague response. I was curious to learn more about his background, but I also sensed it wasn't the right time to dig deeper.

"So, where do we start?" I asked once everything was unloaded in our garage. I knew a fair amount about PCs. After doing a lot of research, I bought the parts for my computer online and then assembled it myself—with a bit of help from my dad and some YouTube tutorials.

"We?" Lucas said, already beginning to disassemble one of the computers using a multi-tool he had brought with him.

"Yeah." I cast a look at Shu and Darian, who appeared to be just as confused as I was. "I thought this was supposed to be a group project."

"I work better on my own," Lucas replied. "So, if you don't mind . . ." His eyes wandered over toward the door that led to our house. As for *my* eyes, they shot wide open in surprise.

"Are you seriously kicking Wyatt out of his own garage?" Darian asked.

Exactly! I thought. The nerve of some people.

Lucas paused what he was doing and fixed his gaze on me. "Do you want to get this squad up and running or not?"

"Of course!"

"Then I don't mean to be rude, but . . ." He tilted his head toward the door again, indicating that the rest of us should vamoose.

Not knowing what else to do, I turned and trudged toward the door, waving for Darian and Shu to follow. "Come on, guys. We might as well get in some practice while we're waiting."

"And if it's not too much trouble," Lucas called out, causing me to pause, my hand on the doorknob, "could you bring me a snack?"

Like I said, the nerve of some people!

- 3 -

While I got out some bread and other fixings to make a sandwich for Lucas—the things I did for that guy!—I seized the opportunity to quiz Darian about his computer. Although he had assured me that his system was ready to go, the more I heard about it, the more concerned I became, especially when he brought up one word in particular.

"Linux?" I asked, hoping I had misheard him.

"Yep," Darian replied. "You know, the open-source operating system."

"I know what Linux is," I replied. "But here's what I don't know. Can you play Rumble Royale on it?"

Darian shrugged. "I don't know. I haven't tried it yet."

"What if you can't?"

"I'm sure we'll figure something out."

"Would you consider installing another operating system, just to be sure?"

"Sorry, no can do," Darian replied. "Technically, it's my parents' computer, and they're hardcore open-source, anti-capitalist, 'information wants to be free' and all that. For them, installing an OS like Windows would be like betraying their deepest values."

Figures, I thought. It fit perfectly with Darian being a vegan and into mindfulness. Nothing about this guy was straight up the middle.

"What are you goons doing in *my* kitchen?" Olivia asked as she swept into the room, her eyes fixed on the island where I was prepping Lucas's snack.

"What does it look like I'm doing?" I replied. "I'm making Lucas a sandwich."

"String Bean?" Her eyes lit up with excitement as she looked around the kitchen for him.

"In garage," Shu said, pointing her thumb in that direction.

BATTLE OF THE BOTS

"Thanks, Shu." Olivia gave her a sweet smile. "I didn't mean to call *you* a goon, by the way." Then she turned to me. "Here, give me that." She reached for the knife I was using. "Who taught you to cut the cheese?"

Darian and I locked eyes in response to her comment, then I turned back to Olivia. "I should have known you'd be an expert on that," I said, holding the knife out to her. "Here, be my guest!"

Olivia's face reddened, then she grinned and

punched me in the shoulder as she realized what she had just said. "You guys are such dorks!"

Darian and I burst out laughing.

Shu smiled, wanting to join in on the fun, but her eyebrows were knit together in confusion. "What so funny?"

The rest of us shared a look, not knowing how to respond. Then a *brraaapp* noise cut through the air. Surprised, I realized that Darian had shoved his arm under his shirt, cupped his hand under his armpit, and then squeezed his other arm down to create a farting sound.

"Cut the cheese," Darian said, then he let loose another ripper. "Get it? Sorry, but I never learned that word in Mandarin."

"Oh," Shu said, nodding and smiling. "Like this?" Before any of us could respond, she stuck her hand under her shirt and let loose a ripper that put Darian's to shame.

"Oh, my gosh, you guys!" Olivia exclaimed as our mouths fell open in shock, then both of us exploded with laughter. "Look at the terrible things you're teaching this poor girl! What will her parents think when she goes back home?"

While Olivia finished preparing Lucas's snack, I took Shu and Darian downstairs so we could go over some basic *Rumble Royale* strategy, starting with the early stages of the game. As I talked, Darian translated for Shu, which I hoped was a step up from the translation app. Then again, I had no idea how fluent in Mandarin he actually was.

"The first thing you need to focus on is getting a good landing," I said as my avatar leaped out of the War Wagon and dove down toward the map. "Be careful not to fly over a mountain or a blimp or anything else that's sticking up high, or it could trigger your glider too early. Like this." I swerved my avatar over a mountain, and my glider, which took the form of a stainless-steel umbrella this time, deployed, slowing my descent.

"Once you get glider locked, there's no going back. So, if your glider deploys too high, everyone else is going to beat you to the ground. See? Like those guys over there."

I pointed to some players as they touched down.

"To make sure that doesn't happen, glide over

water for as long as possible. And don't wait until the War Wagon is right over your landing spot before you jump. Hop out a bit before that, dive down, and then glide. Got it?"

I looked at Shu and Darian, who both nodded in reply, their eyes fixed on my monitor.

"Once you do come in for a landing," I continued as my avatar neared the ground, "keep an eye on your landing spot to see how many other people are there and where they're going. For example, if the spot where you're landing has a blue house, a green house, and a yellow house, and the other players run into the blue and green houses, don't follow them or they'll kill you because they'll get all the guns first. Instead, run into the yellow house and start looting.

"Of course, if *you* land first, you won't be able to see where the other players are, but that won't matter because you'll be able to get loot—including guns—much faster than they will, so they shouldn't be a problem anyway.

"By the way, if you have a choice between landing on a weapon or a chest, go for the weapon because that's a guaranteed gun. The chest may contain a better gun, but it takes time to open the chest, and while that's happening, someone could shoot you. Speaking of shooting..."

I paused as my avatar ran into a gas station, then raced around in search of loot. I found a chest that gave me an AR (assault rifle), some ammo, and other goodies. "You should avoid fights as much as possible early in the game. That's when the things are the most unpredictable—not to mention the most dangerous—because finding guns and other loot at this stage is more a matter of chance than skill. If you're lucky, things could work out in your favor, but they can also turn against you in a hurry.

"If you do have to fight, keep your eyes and ears open for other players sneaking up on you so you don't get so focused on the fight that you wind up getting third-partied—killed by another player. But if you get a chance to third-party someone else, go for it.

"Also, take advantage of NPCs—non-player characters—and vending machines that you can buy things from. It's a great way to pick up a good weapon and heals early on."

As Darian finished translating that last part for Shu, I glanced up from the game and realized she was taking notes on her phone. I couldn't help but smile. She was already my star student. Not wanting to overwhelm them, I decided to bring the lesson to a close.

"One last thing. It's fine to land at a different spot on the map every game when you're starting out so you can familiarize yourself with the entire island, but once you have a good feel for the map, choose a handful of drop points and land at each one several times until you have a good sense of what sort of loot is there and how to use it to your advantage. Any questions?"

Shu held up her left index finger, her eyes fixed on her phone as her right thumb flashed back and forth across the screen. While she finished taking notes, I heard footsteps thumping down the stairs. They were far too heavy for Olivia, so I knew it could only be one other person.

"Finished!" Lucas shouted the moment his tousled hair came into view.

BATTLE OF THE BOTS

Did he eat his snack already? I wondered. *Surely he isn't coming down to ask for more!*

"Finished what?" I asked, already certain I knew the answer.

"The first computer."

"What?" Darian and I said in unison, our mouths falling open in shock for the second time that day.

"Come see for yourself!" Lucas replied, already bounding back up the stairs.

Without a moment's hesitation, Shu, Darian, and I took off after him.

- 4 -

When we reached the garage, we were surprised to find a computer up and running on my dad's workbench. The case was rusty, and the monitor had a couple of lines of burnt-out pixels running across it, but there was no mistaking the Microsoft Windows logo glowing at the center of the screen.

"That's amazing!" Darian said. "How'd you do it so quickly?"

Lucas shrugged as if it was no big deal, wolfing down the remainder of his sandwich and chasing it with a slurp of Coke before replying. "It was pretty easy, actually. I just had to swap the power

supply and graphics card from one computer to another. I also transferred the hard drive from a third computer. It's solid state, if you can believe that. One terabyte. You'd have to be crazy to throw one of those away. And it even came preloaded with Windows Eleven."

"What about the RAM?" I asked as I peered into the case to inspect the machine's innards, still not believing this Frankencomputer idea would actually work. "And the graphics card?"

"It's got eight gigs of RAM, an Intel HD 4000

graphics card, and a 3.3 gigahertz i3 processor," Lucas said, crossing his arms in satisfaction. "Any other questions, Mr. Geek Squad?"

"Hmph," I replied, not wanting to give Lucas the satisfaction of my approval. "Those are the *minimum* requirements to run Rumble Royale. If we hope to compete with the big boys, we'll have to do better than that."

"Yeah, but we have to start somewhere, right?" Darian said, always the peacemaker. He turned to Lucas. "You did an amazing job. What are the chances of you building a second computer out of the rest of the parts for Shu?"

Lucas downed the last of his Coke, wiped his lips on the back of his hand, then shook his head. "No can do. I already used the best of what we had. The rest of what we brought home is basically garbage."

"Well, what's Shu supposed to do?" I asked, as if it was Lucas's fault.

"We could always make another trip to the dump," Darian suggested.

"No way," I said, shaking my head. "We barely got away with it the first time. Besides, my parents are pretty nice, but they won't let us continue filling their garage with junk."

"What matter?" Shu asked, looking back and forth between our faces as she tried to follow the conversation.

Darian explained the situation to her in Mandarin—at least, that's what I *assumed* he was doing. But when she laughed in reply, I began to have my doubts.

"What's so funny?" I asked. Rather than responding to me, Shu said something to Darian in Mandarin. When he heard what she had to say, he broke into laughter too.

"Seriously, guys, what's so funny?" I said, a smile tugging at my face, even though my patience was wearing thin.

In response, Shu opened her wallet, then pulled something out and held it up for us to see.

"A credit card?" I said. "What's so funny about that?"

"It's her parents' credit card," Darian explained. "They sent it with her when she came over here for school, just in case. She says she doesn't have to get a computer from the dump.

She can buy whatever she needs."

Shu said something else to Darian in Mandarin, which caused his eyebrows to shoot up in surprise and his smile to widen even further. "Shu says she can buy the rest of us computers as well, if we want. There's no need for any of us to use a piece of junk like this. Her parents own a factory in Hong Kong that makes baseball caps, if you can believe it. Her family is loaded."

All I could do was shake my head in wonder as I stared at Shu's grinning face. This girl was full of surprises.

"Why didn't she tell us that *before* we went rooting around in the dump?" I asked, speaking to Darian but directing my question to Shu.

Once he translated for her, she turned to me and smiled. "Fun adventure. Want to see what find."

While the three of us were bubbling with excitement, I failed to notice that Lucas was abnormally silent. Rather than weighing in with his opinion, as he usually did, he was typing into his phone.

"What do you say, Lucas?" I asked. "Do you want Shu to buy you a computer?"

BATTLE OF THE BOTS

Lucas finished what he was typing. Then he started shutting down the computer. "Why would I want her to do that?" he asked.

"Look at this thing," I said as the monitor flashed and glitched. "I mean, I'm amazed you found *anything* worth keeping from that pile of trash we hauled home, let alone something that—"

"One person's trash is another person's treasure," Lucas said, glaring up at me from the keyboard. "Ever heard that saying before?"

"Yes, but—"

"Well, not everyone gets everything handed to them on a silver platter. This may seem like a piece of junk to a rich kid like you, Wyatt, but it's the first computer I've ever owned. So, thanks for the kind offer, Shu, but this setup will suit me just fine."

While Lucas finished unplugging everything and wrapping up the cords, the rest of us remained silent, our eyes on the floor as his words sank in. My family wasn't rich, but we weren't exactly hurting for money either. Neither was Darian's family, by the sound of it. As for Shu—well, her unlimited credit card spoke for itself.

For the second time, it occurred to me that Lucas might have it a lot harder than the rest of us. Suddenly, I felt terrible for bringing him down to my gaming room, which was maxed out with all the latest gadgets. Did he think I had done it just to rub it in his face? No wonder he had been so concerned about getting his share of the prize money, not to mention all the food he ate whenever he came over to my house.

"Lucas, I'm sorry," I said. "I didn't think—"

"It doesn't matter," Lucas said as he hit the button for the overhead garage door.

"Where are you going?" I asked, raising my voice as the door clacked open on its track.

"Someone's coming to pick me up."

"Who?" Darian asked.

Before Lucas could reply, the roar of a car's engine filled our ears, followed by the shriek of squealing tires. Seconds later, a rusted-out mid-1990s Volkswagen Jetta lurched to a stop in our driveway, roaring and smoking as the driver pumped the gas pedal, probably to keep the engine from dying.

BATTLE OF THE BOTS

I tried to see who was inside, but due to the car's tinted windows and the reflections on the windshield, it was impossible.

"It's my older brother," Lucas said on his way out. "And probably some of his friends."

"Don't you want to stick around and practice?" I shouted over the car's roaring engine and the heavy metal music blasting from inside.

"I can practice at home," Lucas replied. "On this!" He waved the keyboard in the air, then opened the car's rear passenger door.

Once Lucas and all his gear were piled inside, the car slammed into reverse and then backed out of our driveway, leaving black marks on the asphalt as it tore down the street in a swirl of smoke and dust.

I waved the clouds of exhaust away from my face as I hit the button to close the garage door, hoping to cut down on the fumes.

"I feel terrible about calling Lucas's computer a piece of junk," Darian said once the door had rattled shut.

"Me too," I replied. "I had no idea his family

had it so rough. Did you see his brother's car? I'm amazed they even allow that thing out on the street."

"It makes me thankful for what I have," Darian said. "I hope that computer really does work for him."

"Yeah, me too," I replied. "Because if it doesn't, he's the kind of guy who'll be too proud to let us know, never mind ask for help."

"Give him time," Darian said. "He likes Shu and your sister, so who knows? Maybe the two of them can get him to reconsider."

"You could be right," I said, my mood brightening at the thought. "So, what should we do now?" I looked at the others for an answer.

Shu smiled and waved her credit card in the air. "Shopping?"

My face broke into a grin. "Great idea!"

- 5 -

By some sort of technological miracle, Lucas managed to boot up his computer again once he got it home, and he was even able to access the Internet and download *Rumble Royale.*

Darian's situation was a bit more complicated. While his computer was light-years ahead of Lucas's setup, before we could even install *Rumble Royale,* we had to install all sorts of other programs, including Lutris and Wine and something called the Heroic Games Launcher. But after a lot of back and forth and arguing, not to mention consulting numerous YouTube tutorials and Reddit posts, we got it up and running.

Compared to Lucas and Darian, getting Shu into the game was a breeze. I could have bought parts online and then assembled a computer for her from scratch, but it was quicker and easier to buy a pre-packaged gaming system. It went against my tech geek instincts, but Shu seemed happy with it, so that was good enough for me.

With everyone online, we could finally do our first team training session—or so I thought until my phone rang. It was Lucas.

"Let me guess. Your computer crashed," I said without even bothering to say hello.

"No, it's my Wi-Fi, actually," Lucas replied. "I'm staying at my mom's house, and she's been leeching Wi-Fi off one of our neighbors for the last several months. But they just got into an argument, so he changed the password, and now I'm locked out."

It was the first time I'd heard Lucas mention that he didn't live with both of his parents—something else I'd assumed was true of most kids just because it was true of me.

"Why doesn't your mom pay for her own Wi-Fi?"

BATTLE OF THE BOTS

"She can't afford it."

I fell silent for a moment, once again feeling stupid for making Lucas have to address the financial gap that existed between us.

"So, what are you going to do?"

"That's why I'm calling," Lucas replied. "Can I bring my computer over to your place?"

Before I responded, I leaned back in my chair and looked around my gaming room. There was plenty of space for Lucas, and I was sure we could round up another desk and chair somewhere. Wi-Fi wouldn't be a problem either. Seeing as my computer was hardwired into our router, having another computer on the system wouldn't slow me down at all. It was spending so much time in the same room with Lucas that gave me pause. Wouldn't we drive each other crazy? I also worried about what it would do to our family's food budget.

Then again, it wasn't like we'd be interacting directly. We'd both have our headsets on and be communicating within the game whether Lucas was in the same room with me or not. So, there really was no difference if he was at his place or mine. But even so . . .

"You still there?" Lucas asked, the sound of his voice making me realize I'd remained silent far longer than I'd intended.

"I guess that's all right," I replied, struggling to keep the reluctance out of my voice. "How soon can you—?"

"On my way!" Lucas said before I could finish my question. Then he hung up.

Twenty minutes later, the roar of his brother's car signaled Lucas's approach. I opened the garage door and let him inside so we could go straight downstairs and avoid a lengthy pit stop in the kitchen visiting with my mom or whoever else was home, but at the top of the stairs, we ran into You-Know-Who.

"String Bean!" Olivia said, her eyes shining with delight when she saw Lucas. "You're back!" When she saw the computer components we were carrying, though, including Lucas's computer case—which he had covered with stickers for various heavy metal groups, probably to hide the rust spots—she drew back in disgust and pointed her finger at it. "What's *that?*"

"What does it look like?" Lucas asked as he sidled past her and headed down the stairs. "You know, I sure could use another one of your wonderful sandwiches!" he called back over his shoulder.

"I don't know, Lucas." I slashed my index finger across my throat and shook my head at Olivia as I struggled to balance Lucas's monitor and keyboard in my arms. "We really don't have—"

"Coming right up!" Olivia shouted, baring her teeth at me in a grin.

"And a Coke if you have it!" Lucas added.

"You got it!" Olivia replied.

I rolled my eyes in defeat and then followed Lucas down the stairs. There was no winning with those two.

Once we had Lucas's computer set up on a card table across the room from mine and he had finished his snack—which included a sandwich plus two oatmeal chocolate chip cookies—we could get down to business. Olivia had been nice enough to bring me one as well, knowing they were my favorite.

"Shu, Darian, are you there?" I said into my

headset. When they both responded in the affirmative, I broke into a grin. "All right, people, it's the moment we've all been waiting for! The inaugural session of the proud and mighty—"

Just then, all three of my computer monitors went black, and the room was plunged into darkness.

"You've got to be kidding me," I said. "Shu, Darian, are you there?"

"They can't hear you," Lucas said. "Looks like the power went out."

"That's just great," I said, tearing off my headset

and tossing it onto my desk. "What are we supposed to do now?"

Lucas leaned back in his chair and shrugged. "We wait. In the meantime, do you think you have any more of those cookies? They're delicious."

I huffed in annoyance. This guy's stomach was bottomless!

As it turned out, we only had to wait about thirty minutes before the power came back on, but that was more than enough time for Lucas to eat not one but three more cookies and down another Coke. I'd hate to see his dentist bill.

As for the power outage, I was worried about what it might have done to Lucas's computer. Mine was plugged into a surge protector just in case of such incidents, but his was plugged straight into the wall.

When Lucas hit the power button to turn his computer back on, I cringed, thinking we were about to witness an explosion of sparks, followed by smoke and a burning smell. If that had happened, I would have been relieved because it would have forced Lucas to accept Shu's offer of a brand-new computer. Instead, it booted up as if nothing out of the ordinary had happened.

"That's my girl," Lucas said, patting the case.

"You gendered your computer?" I asked, smirking.

"I didn't just give her a gender. I gave her a name too," Lucas replied as he typed in his password.

"Which is . . .?"

"None of your business," he replied.

"You named your computer 'None of Your Business'?"

I know, cheeky.

He flashed a half smirk at me and then put on his headset. "That was almost funny, Wyatt. Now, what are you waiting for?"

Realizing I had yet to boot up my computer, I ran over to it, and in no time I was back up and running as well.

"Okay, boys and girl," I said. "Let's get this party started!"

- 6 -

I'd assumed that once we had everyone online at the same time, we could start training for real. But as I was learning, nothing was simple and straightforward with this group.

Our first hurdle? Choosing a skin or a character to play in the game.

"It really doesn't matter which skin you choose," I said for what felt like the twentieth time. "Even though some people think certain skins give you an advantage, that isn't true. The hitbox—the spot where an attack will do damage—is the same size no matter what skin you use."

"What about blending into the environment?" Darian asked. "Don't some skins offer you better camouflage than others?"

"Maybe at a distance, but the more you play the game, the more you'll realize that's only effective if you're standing still, and when it comes to Rumble Royale, you're rarely standing still."

Just then, a familiar voice sounded in my headset. I recognized it all too well, but I had no idea why I was hearing it at that moment.

"Oliva? Is that you?"

"You'd better believe it," she replied.

"But what . . . where are you? And how did you get online with us?"

"I'm at Shu's house."

"You're where? But you were just—"

"She invited me to come over while you guys train today so I could help her pick an outfit for her avatar."

"But how did you—?"

"Mom drove me."

I sighed, then returned to the subject at hand. "They're called *skins*," I said, trying to keep the growl out of my voice for Shu's sake, "not 'outfits.'"

"Whatever you call them, I just wanted to make sure Shu doesn't get stuck with something ugly."

I heard some murmuring as she and Shu discussed some options away from the mic. Then Olivia came back on. "Okay, I think we got it. What do you guys think?"

Moments later, Shu's avatar joined us in the lobby. The skin she chose was a girl with long dark hair dressed in a green jumpsuit and goggles. Her avatar's sledgehammer looked like a meat cleaver.

"Pretty cool, right?" Oliva said.

"Where'd you find that skin?" Lucas asked. "I don't see it as an option in my locker."

"That's because you need to buy it," I said. "If you want something other than the default skins, you either have to buy them in the item shop or buy a battle pass. Then every time you level up, you'll earn battle stars, which let you unlock rewards, including skins."

"Well, I don't like any of the default skins," Lucas said.

"Neither do I," Darian added.

I muted my mic so I could let out a long, withering growl without anyone hearing it—except possibly Lucas, who was in the same room with his back to me. Then I turned my mic back on. "Like I said, guys, the type of skin you use doesn't matter."

"Maybe not to you," Lucas replied.

I growled again. This time I didn't bother to mute my mic.

"Good news, guys," Olivia said. "Shu says she's willing to buy the rest of you any skin you want!"

"Really, Shu, you don't have to—"

"That's great!" Lucas shouted. For a guy who had refused to accept charity from Shu before, I was surprised at how quickly he agreed to the offer. Darian thanked Shu but said he could buy his own skin. I already had dozens of skins—I'd spent way too much of my allowance on them—so I told her I didn't need any help in that department either.

So, rather than getting into a game, the next fifteen minutes were taken up by Lucas examining and then rejecting dozens of skins. I was amazed at how quickly he could riffle through them. Eventually, he whittled it down to three options, which he sent to everyone else on our Stream Team Discord server so we could cast our vote.

However, in typical Lucas fashion, the second we gave our feedback, he rejected all three of those options and went with a fourth one—a tough-looking avatar in gray plate-mail armor with a massive golden sledgehammer. It looked like exactly the sort of skin a *Warhammer* player would choose.

As for Darian, he went with a ninja-type skin. His costume was purple, and the lower part of his face was covered by a mask. His sledgehammer took the form of a bo staff.

"What about you, Wyatt?" Darian asked.

"Yeah, Wyatt," Olivia said. "What are you going to go with? That secret agent guy with the tattoos and the golden sledgehammer you think makes you look so cool?"

"You do know we can change our skins any time we want, right?" I said. "It's not like we have to stick with the same ones for every game."

"But if we want to build a brand, an identity, especially when we start streaming, it's important that we have a consistent look, isn't it?" Lucas argued.

I widened my eyes in annoyance, thankful the rest of the team couldn't see me. "I guess so. But it's not so much our skins that will set us apart but how well we—"

"Then it's settled," Lucas said before I could finish. "Whatever skin we choose today, that's what we stick with from now on. Everyone agreed?"

"Yes," Darian replied.

"Agreed!" Oliva and Shu said in unison, followed by a giggle.

I glared back over my shoulder. Why was it that every time I tried to do something, Lucas took control, and the rest of the team was so quick to follow him?

"So, what's it going to be, Wyatt?" Lucas asked. "The clock is ticking."

"Fine," I said. "You want our team to have a distinct identity? Here it is." Rather than choosing the skin Olivia mentioned—which really did look pretty cool, like James Bond combined with an emo vampire—I went in the opposite direction just to spite her and Lucas.

"Are you serious?" Olivia asked. "You want to

become a famous gamer known around the world as *that* guy?"

"What's wrong with it?" I turned my avatar in a circle. He was dressed in a red vest, green pants, and metal shin guards, and he had a jack o'lantern on his head. His sledgehammer was shaped like a farmer's spiked club.

"You seriously want to go with that?" Lucas asked, taking off his headset and turning to face me.

"Why not?" I asked, taking off my headset and doing the same. "Not cool enough for you? Should we put it to a vote?"

He shrugged and then put his headset back on. "Suit yourself."

I took a moment to think about it. I'll be the first to admit that skin wasn't my top choice, but if it irritated Lucas, that was good enough for me.

"If the fashion show's over, can we finally play a game?" I asked.

"Let's do it!" Darian said.

"Hold your horses!" Lucas cut in. "We need to do one more thing first."

"What could that possibly be?" I asked, almost

at the end of my rope.

"What do you think, *KwyattWyatt?*" Lucas replied. "Gamertags!"

Groaning inwardly, I expected the gamertag discussion to take at least another thirty minutes, if not longer, but unlike the skins debate, it was surprisingly fast.

Once again, Shu went first. "Introducing . . . TheShuTangClan," Olivia said, making Shu's announcement for her.

"Not bad, not bad," Lucas said. "Sort of like the hip-hop group. How about you, Darian?"

"I thought I'd go with TaterThought," Darian replied. "Might as well keep things consistent, right?"

"I love it," Lucas said, as if he were the one who had to approve every decision. Why wasn't anyone asking what I thought?

"What about you, Lucas?" I asked, part of me ready to dispute whichever one he chose, even if I thought it was cool.

"Believe it or not, I've put a lot of thought into this," Lucas began, the tone of his voice making it sound like he was about to launch into a long explanation of the various options he had considered and then discarded before announcing his gamertag of choice. Hoping to cut him off at the pass, I jumped in.

"So, what is it?"

"Do you really want to know?" Lucas asked, a smile in his voice.

"Yes!" I cried. "Anything so we can get on with our training."

"Okay, you asked for it, and here it is . . . WarHammerHead. You like it?"

I paused to think. It actually wasn't bad, and it fit Lucas perfectly.

"I like it," Darian said. "But I'm amazed no one has thought about it before. Are you sure it isn't already taken?"

"It is now," Lucas replied. "By me."

"Alrighty then," I said. "We have our skins—for now—and our gamertags. Is there anything else we need before we jump into our first game together? Anyone need to go to the bathroom? Grab a snack?"

"Actually . . ."

"I was only kidding about the snack!" I said before Lucas could continue. "Now, let's go!"

- 7 -

"Mic check. Everyone here?" I asked once we were all in the War Wagon and heading into our first battle royale as a squad. "Sound off just to be sure."

Seeing as the others had only ever played solo, before we jumped out of the War Wagon, I decided it was a good time to share some strategies for how to fight together as a squad.

"First of all, working as a team is the key to success. There's no room for any lone wolves out there. I'm looking at you, Lucas," I said, glancing over my shoulder at him.

"Hey," Lucas protested, pretending to be offended.

"For starters, that means coordinating our landing, ideally in the same building. There won't be as much loot to go around, but it'll allow us to rush any other teams that have split up.

"If you do happen to wander off and get yourself killed, tell the rest of us where you were eliminated. Then we'll know where to go if we decide to revive you."

"*If?*" Darian said. "Why wouldn't you revive a dead player?"

"If we're in the middle of a firefight, sometimes

it's better to take out the other team first so the rest of us don't get killed too. And if the rest of us are getting our butts kicked, we might have to book it and leave you behind."

"Got it."

"I want to hear lots of communication out there," I continued. "Keep talking. And keep your eyes peeled. Make sure your visual footsteps setting is on, and be aware of your surroundings at all times. Look for signs of other players building or trees falling down as people loot from them. And *never* run into a building without scouting it first. If you spot other squads or individual players nearby, let the rest of us know, and we can decide *as a group* if we want to attack or retreat."

"Shu wants to know how we decide when to fight and when to run."

I frowned in surprise at the sound of my sister's voice. "Olivia? Are you still online?"

"Of course!"

Shaking my head, I was about to answer Shu's question when I realized it was time to jump out of the War Wagon.

"Here we go," I said. "Jump! Let's head to Rockface Lodge. Everyone follow me, and don't deploy your glider until I say so."

"Why are we going there?" Lucas asked. "Why not Cunningham Keep or Windermere? I like the sound of those places."

That figured. Of all the spots on the map, they sounded the most like place names from *Warhammer*.

"Because those are two of the most popular spots, and we want to go someplace where hardly any other teams will be."

"Is there even any good loot there?" Lucas asked, his voice full of doubt. "It sounds like a country club where old men with white mustaches and cardigan sweaters smoke cigars as they talk about their latest fox hunt."

"It's got plenty of loot," I replied. "Every place on the map does."

"But some places must be better than others," Lucas insisted.

"Of course they are! But this is just a training run, okay? So, let's keep things simple."

"All right, all right, no need to freak out."

"I'm not freaking out!"

"Um, it sounds like you are, Wyatt," Olivia said.

"So much for the 'Kwyatt' part," Lucas quipped.

My brain was scrambling for a witty reply when I realized I had been so caught up in arguing with Lucas that I almost lost track of where we were. "Quick, deploy your gliders!" I said as I deployed mine. "And follow me!"

In keeping with my bucket-head scarecrow character, my glider took the form of a straw bale. Shu's looked like a bullet with crisscrossing white stripes that matched her outfit. Lucas's glider was covered with glowing blue spikes, just like his armor, and Darian's was in the shape of an origami swan.

"Um . . . Shu's still waiting for you to answer the question," Olivia said.

"What question?" I asked, so focused on coordinating our jump that I had forgotten all about it.

"When to run and when to fight?"

"Oh, yeah. If we outnumber the other team, we play aggressively. We attack any team that's split up. That'll force them to decide whether to revive the dead player or continue the fight. The same goes for any player who's flanking us or out of position. Light 'em up."

"Got it."

"And if we're the ones getting ambushed, stick together. If one of us gets shot and needs to heal or build up their shields, the rest of us can build around them and provide cover. Okay, folks, here we go!"

Rather than landing right on Rockface Lodge, we hit the ground on a brown hill sticking up out of the snow-covered landscape. After sliding down, I raced toward the building.

"See that van with the curved blue arrow swirling over it?" I asked as my avatar ran past.

"You'd have to be blind not to," Lucas replied.

I rolled my eyes and then continued my explanation. "That's a rez van. If one of us dies, someone else needs to grab their rez card and then take it to the van."

"Is there just one rez van?" Darian asked.

"No, they're scattered all over the map. But you have to be careful when using them. It takes ten seconds to rez, and some teams like to stake them out, sniping anyone who tries."

"Right," Darian replied. "Makes sense."

"Now, follow me inside," I said as I approached the lodge, which was made of dark wooden beams with white plaster walls and was surrounded by a low boxwood hedge.

"Looks puny," Lucas said.

"That's because it is!" I replied. "But there'll be plenty of good loot inside. Trust me."

I ran through the front door, the others right behind me.

The main floor was open concept, featuring a large kitchen and dining room.

"Someone grab that med kit," I said as I ran past it toward a closed door. "Actually, we should assign one person to carry most of the heals and another person to carry the shields."

"I'll handle the heals," Darian said, which seemed fitting considering his focus on mindfulness and well-being.

"Sounds good," I replied. "We'll make you the team medic."

"I like it!"

"Shu says she'll carry the shields," Olivia added.

"Okay," I replied.

In the bedroom, I found a decent gun and some ammo.

"Got a weapon," I said. "Why don't we all split up and search the rest of the house so the rest of you can find guns too? It'll go quicker that way." Normally, a single building wouldn't have enough loot to outfit an entire squad, but this place was like a small hotel with plenty of rooms.

"But you just said no lone wolves," Lucas reminded me. "Remember?"

"I realize that. But as long as we're all in the same building, it's fine. Look everywhere—behind doors, under the stairs, on the balcony, and on the roof. And feel free to smash whatever you see with your sledgehammer. Not only will it allow you to loot wood and other materials, but chests and other goodies are often hidden inside other things, like stoves and closets. But don't smash all the way through the walls or we'll have no protection if another squad rolls up on us."

BATTLE OF THE BOTS

As my teammates ran around scouring the place for loot, I followed them to make sure they found everything and that no one hoarded shields, ammo, or heals.

"Remember, sharing is caring, guys. The more members of our team are alive, the better our chances at winning a match. So, keeping everyone's health and shields topped up is better than just one of us being at full strength. Got it?"

"Roger," Darian replied.

"Ditto," Lucas added. "Um, is it okay that I just knocked a hole in the roof? I got a little carried away with my sledgehammer up here."

"That's fine," I said. "Once you're all finished looting, let's meet on the main floor so we can redistribute everything and max out our shields."

"Um, does anyone else hear that?" Olivia asked.

"Hear what?" I replied, only to realize a second later what she was talking about.

Gunshots.

"I'm hit!" Lucas cried.

- 8 -

"How'd they manage to sneak up on us?" Darian yelled, his voice filled with panic. "And how did they know we were here?"

"They probably crouch walked," I said. "That way, you don't make any sound when you move. As for how they found us, someone was bound to check out this building sooner or later, but Lucas blowing a hole in our roof with his sledgehammer probably didn't help. Lucas, how much damage did you take?"

"I'm not sure, but all I can do right now is crawl around on the floor."

BATTLE OF THE BOTS

"That means you've been knocked. They probably nailed you with a head shot. If we leave you like that for too long, you're going to die. Where are you?"

"On the second floor, near the top of the stairs. I think they shot me through a window."

"Okay, sit tight," I said. "The rest of you, get up to the second floor—now! It'll be the easiest place to defend in case they decide to attack us."

Once everyone was at the top of the stairs, I used my sledgehammer to knock out the ceiling and then boxed up, creating enough of a structure that the other team would have to break or shoot through a lot of layers before they got to us. Thankfully, I'd scrounged up enough mats while looting the lodge to do it, but now I was pretty much tapped out.

"Anyone find a Sizzle Drink, a Sling Splash, or anything like that?" I asked.

"Shu wants to know what those look like," Olivia said. I was really hoping Shu would start speaking for herself at some point, but at the moment, there was no time to argue.

"Like a six-pack of energy drinks or four bottles of juice," I replied.

"I've got a Sling Splash!" Darian said.

"Good. Throw it at Lucas. That'll buy him some time."

"Um, how?"

"Hold down your right mouse button to aim it at Lucas, then click your left mouse button."

A second later, Darian did exactly that, but instead of throwing the Sling Splash at Lucas, it exploded on the ceiling of our box instead.

"Oops," Darian said. "Sorry."

"I'm dying over here!" Lucas cried.

"Chill out," I said. "You only lose two ticks per second. That shot took you down to one hundred units of health, which means we've got fifty seconds to revive you. Anyone else have any heals?"

My question was met with dead silence—apart from Lucas counting down his health status.

"Forty-six . . . forty-four . . ."

"Okay, I guess we'll just wait for him to die then," I said.

"What?" Lucas exclaimed.

"I mean, one of us could revive you by holding down the same button you use to pick up weapons and open chests and stuff, but this'll be good practice. Don't worry. It doesn't mean you'll be out of the game. As soon as you're dead, one of us can run your rez card to the van and revive you. While we're waiting for Lucas to tap out, the rest of you, down whatever you've got to boost your shields, and keep a lookout for the other team."

"Why haven't they attacked us?" Darian asked.

"Forty . . . thirty-eight . . ."

"They probably just took a pot shot at Lucas as they were running past," I said.

"Or maybe they're waiting outside, ready to ambush us as soon as we come out," Olivia suggested.

"Possibly," I replied. "It's definitely too risky for them to come into the building and fight us, especially this early in the game. Not that we have much to fight them with, but they don't know that. Anyway, we'd better hope they're not out there because as soon as we revive Lucas, we'll have to book it. The zone's going to shift soon."

We waited until Lucas's health hit zero. Then I

grabbed his rez card and used my sledgehammer to smash through the walls I'd just built.

"Shu, follow me so you can cover me while I wait beside the rez van. It takes ten seconds to rez someone. Darian, go out a different door. That way, if someone's waiting outside to ambush us, they won't be able to get all three of us at once, and maybe you can get the drop on them. And while you're waiting for us to finish, loot whatever mats you can so we'll have something to build with in case we get into a fight on our way to the next safe zone."

"Roger," Darian replied.

With Shu hard on my heels, I raced downstairs and peeked out the front door.

"I don't see anyone, Shu. Do you?"

"No!" It was Shu speaking this time instead of Olivia. What a relief.

"Okay, I'm going to make a run for the van. Cover me!"

I dashed outside to the rez van. Before I inserted Lucas's card, I used the last of my mats to throw a wooden wall on the side of me that was facing away from Shu. It wasn't much, but at least it would give me some protection in case anyone took a shot at me. I wished I had thought to ask someone to give me some brick or something so I could box myself in completely. I felt like a total bot sitting out there with virtually no protection. All I could do was hope that the other teams were in a hurry to get to the new zone as well.

"Hurry!" Lucas said.

"I'm going as fast as I can!"

As soon as I inserted his rez card, the van started to hum, and a blue light began to travel around the curved arrow on the side of the van. It was like a progress bar on a computer, and just like every other progress bar I'd ever been forced to watch, it couldn't go fast enough.

"Almost there," I said as the light reached the halfway point.

"Can't you make it go any faster?" Lucas asked.

"What do *you* think?" I said, my exasperation reaching the breaking point.

Just then my controller buzzed so hard, I almost dropped it, and the sound of a shotgun blast rippled through my ear canals.

"No!" I wailed in disbelief as my avatar fell to its knees beside the rez van. "I've been knocked!"

A moment later, a player whose skin resembled the plant-faced monster from *Stranger Things* jumped out and finished me off with another shotgun blast.

"That one-pump chump was hiding in the bush!"

"Now what are we going to do?" Lucas yelled. "He's going to kill me as soon as I revive!"

"Not if I have anything to say about it," Darian replied, a steely hardness in his voice that I'd never heard before. "Take that!"

As the kid who killed me scooped up my loot, he got absolutely lasered by Darian, who jumped out from beside Rockface Lodge. Even Shu managed to hit him once, having stepped out of her hiding spot in the building at the same time.

"Nailed him!" Lucas said as his avatar jumped down from on top of the rez van, where he had respawned.

"Careful!" I warned. "His teammates could be hiding around here too."

"Why do you assume it's a 'he'?" Olivia asked.

BATTLE OF THE BOTS

Just then an alarm sounded, indicating the storm circle was about to start shrinking.

"I don't have time for questions!" I said. "Someone grab my rez card and stick it in the—"

My voice was drowned out by an explosion of gunfire.

"Ambush!" Lucas yelled.

"Run!" I said.

"But your rez card!" Olivia cried.

"Just leave it or you're all going to die!"

- 9 -

I watched in horror as the remainder of my squad leaped and ran across the map while the other team gave chase, bullets flying in every direction. I thought I was only seconds away from watching them all die.

Thankfully, the other team had about as much shooting skill as the average stormtrooper, which meant they wouldn't have been able to hit the rear end of an elephant with a water balloon if it was standing right in front of them.

While I was glad to see my teammates escape, I couldn't believe we had just begun our first real mission, and I was already dead! That wasn't exactly going to fill my fellow players with confidence about my abilities.

Even though I was out of the game, I figured I could still coach them. Now that I wasn't paying attention to my own actions, it actually made it a little easier to focus on the others.

"As soon as you're all in the circle, find some high ground and then box up so you can catch your breath," I said. "Does everyone remember how to box up?"

"I think so," Darian replied. "I'm pretty low on mats, though."

"Then box up next to a tree or a big rock. Once you're under cover, you can mine the rock or the tree to replace what you just used."

"Good thinking," Darian said.

"It's actually a pretty basic strategy," Lucas pointed out. He couldn't help but show off his knowledge at every turn.

"It may be basic, but you'll be thankful for the extra mats in case someone shoots out one of your walls," I said.

While I waited for them to get set up, I glanced at the counter that showed how many squads were remaining. Each battle royale began with twenty-five four-person squads. Even if only one member of a squad was still alive, their team still showed up on the counter.

"Twenty squads left," I announced, "which means nineteen other squads—or parts of squads—are still out there."

"And if we eliminate them all, we win?" Darian asked.

"Something like that." I couldn't believe he thought that was even a remote possibility, especially with me no longer in the game, but I admired his optimism.

"Should one of us run back and get your rez card, Wyatt?" Olivia asked. "We really could use your help."

"I'm touched that you'd think of me, little sister, but no, the storm would kill you long before you got there and back."

"So, what are we supposed to do?"

"Start kicking butts and taking names!" Lucas

yelled, causing me to wince and turn down the volume in my headset.

"Actually, you guys are low on pretty much everything, including ammo, so I suggest you focus on looting before the circle moves again. Two of you can loot while the other stands watch. I'll leave it to you guys to decide who does what."

"Who's got the most ammo?" Darian asked. "That person should stand guard."

"I have lots," Shu said.

"Okay, Shu. Keep your eyes peeled while Darian and I slash and burn this place."

Lucas had a tendency to make everything sound as dramatic as possible.

"I'll be an extra set of eyes and ears," I said, scanning my monitor for any signs of other players in the distance. I saw a box fight taking place in the top-right corner of my screen, but they were far away and too busy fighting each other to notice our squad as they hacked at trees, trucks, fences, rocks, and anything else they could find in the immediate area.

"Here's a pro tip," I said as Lucas whacked at a

tree. "It's okay to farm wood from trees, but don't break them completely. If someone sees the tree fall, you'll be a sitting duck for a sneak attack."

"Got it," Lucas replied as he finished the tree off, causing it to explode in a shower of sparks and wood chips.

"I thought I just told you not to do that," I said.

"Sorry. I like the sound it makes."

I closed my eyes and rubbed my temples in frustration. "Anyway..."

Just then an alarm sounded, signaling the next zone shift. I looked at the preview of where the next circle would be. Unfortunately, it couldn't have been farther away from where our team was.

"Okay, guys, we got a bad pull. Split up whatever mats and heals you've managed to gather and then I suggest you start rotating," I said. "The zone is going to pull to the north, and you're all the way on the south side. Lots of other teams are probably stuck in the same position, so you want to get there ahead of them. If you can find a good spot to box up inside the zone, preferably on some high ground, maybe you can pick off a few stragglers on their way in."

"Roger," Darian replied. I really liked how he took direction. He was so teachable, unlike other people I could name . . .

"Wait a second. I want to check out this fishing shack over here first," Lucas said.

As his avatar ran toward the shack, which was located beside a lake, I saw that it was surrounded by the remnants of someone else's builds.

"Don't bother," I said. "A fight already went down there. I'm sure the place was looted already. Plus, you never know who might be lingering inside, waiting for some noob like you to show up."

"A little peek won't hurt," Lucas said.

"Actually, in Rumble Royale, a peek could get you killed," I replied.

"Yeah, Lucas," Darian added. "Pigs get slaughtered, remember? Don't get greedy. We need to stick together, bro. You've already died once."

"You heard the boss, String Bean. Get out of there."

I don't need to tell you who said that.

"Oh, all right," Lucas said. "You bunch of chickens."

The team managed to rotate without getting killed or even encountering any other players, so there was no need to get into a fight or use many of their mats except when they boxed up. Apart from a bit of confusion about which buttons to press when boxing up, they pulled that part off pretty well too.

After they survived through a few more zone shifts, their building skills improving each time, I figured they were ready for me to shake things up a bit. Besides, I was getting bored just watching.

"Okay," I said, "you all have a pretty good inventory of mats and plenty of heals, so it's time to stop looting and shift to the best part of this game ... fighting."

- 10 -

"You mean you actually want us to go looking for a fight?" Darian asked. "Isn't it a bit early in the game to do that?"

"Normally, I'd agree," I replied. "You should avoid fights during midgame, which is pretty much where we are right now, because it could scuff you for endgame, which is when you want full materials and full health. But seeing as this is just a training run, I think you should go for it."

"Finally!" Lucas exclaimed.

"But you'll have to be careful," I warned. "By this point, everyone else is probably all stocked up too. And you guys are down one player, which makes you vulnerable to a full squad. Ideally, we need to find a team with only one or two players still alive and see if we can ambush them. The good thing is, seeing as most other players will be trying to avoid fights at this stage, they'll assume you guys will be too, so their guard will be down, and they won't expect an attack."

"Shu wants to know what the word 'ambush' means," Olivia said. "To be honest, so do I. Does it have anything to do with trees?"

"Um, excuse me?" I said, more than a little confused.

"You know, am*bush,* as in bushes?"

"Oh, well, that's not what I—"

"It could definitely involve a literal bush," Lucas cut in. "Exactly the way I just died. But to answer your question, in general, to ambush someone doesn't have anything to do with trees. It means to launch a surprise attack from a concealed position. Keep going, Wyatt."

"Uh, thanks," I said, surprised at Lucas being so quick to hand over the mic. "Yeah, you can definite-

BATTLE OF THE BOTS

ly ambush someone by hiding in an actual bush, as we just saw with Lucas, but that won't work for an entire squad. There are a few other things that will work, though.

"The first is to use the terrain against your opponents. For example, if you get to the top of a cliff and see someone fishing on the beach below, if you open fire, the only way they can escape is to swim—which makes them extremely vulnerable because they can't shoot back. Either that or they'll have to build their way out, which'll force them to use up their mats and make them vulnerable when and if they survive to endgame. If you all concentrate your fire on one player, that will separate them from their teammates, who will be too focused on running away and healing to put up much of a fight.

"Another option is to choose a closed-in area, like under a bridge, ideally with a hill or some other obstacle on one side, and then stake it out, waiting for other players to wander in. Then as you open fire on them, they'll be trapped.

"A third way is to third party someone. Find

two teams that are already engaged in a fight and then sneak up on them. Once again, the key is for the entire squad to concentrate their fire on the same person, or it won't work. That means you need to communicate with each other at all times, and stick together. Even if you spot someone while you're on your own and you have a clear shot, wait for your teammates to catch up first. Got it?"

"Yes," Darian replied.

"Shu is nodding," Olivia said.

"Lucas?"

"What?"

"Did you hear what I just said?"

"Sorry, I was texting someone. Can you repeat everything after the whole 'hiding in a bush' part?"

I spun around in my desk chair and glared at Lucas, only to be greeted by his trademark smirk.

I pulled my headset away from my right ear. "Seriously?"

His smile widened further. "Just kidding!"

I shook my head in annoyance and then turned back to my monitor. "While it's important to work as a team, sometimes if you wait too long you'll miss the opportunity, so use your best judgment. The goal with any ambush is to do a boatload of damage to your opponents *before* they know you're there. That's what'll give you the edge. If you rush it, you could find yourself in a box fight, using up all your heals and builds and ammo. And if the players you're fighting are better than you, they could turn the tables and kill you instead. All right, now that you all know the basics, let's go hunting!"

I scanned the map, looking for a spot where there was a high probability they'd get into a fight. "Let's head over to Hasty Railways," I said. "It's one of the most popular landing spots, seeing as it's close to the middle of the island and full of loot. However, rather than running straight into town, see these mountains here?" I pinged them on the map, which created a blue beacon extending into the sky, making it easy for the other players to find it. "Let's come at it from that direction. It'll give you the high ground and a bit of cover. With any luck, you might find someone who's still looting there and get the drop on them."

I waited until the squad was in position and

then leaned back in my chair, removing my hand from my mouse and crossing my arms. "Okay, I'm going to let the three of you handle things on your own from here. Lucas, you're the strategy guy. Why don't you take the lead?"

"Gladly. Anything to get your whiny little voice out of my head."

I growled into my mic before muting it, the other players laughing at Lucas's remark and my response.

"Okay, people," Lucas said. "What are we seeing down there?"

"Lots of pretty buildings?" Olivia replied.

"Look like Italy," Shu added.

"I wasn't exactly looking for a review from Architectural Digest, but thanks for playing. I meant tactically. Darian?"

"I think I just saw someone run into the train station!" Darian cried.

"Good," Lucas said. "That's something we can use. Anything else?"

There was a pause as the other players scoped out the situation.

"I don't think so," Olivia replied.

"It's like a ghost town down there," Darian added.

"That's what worries me," Lucas said. "But there's not much we can do from up here, and the clock is ticking, so let's head down there and see if we can take that kid out."

"I just hope his big brother isn't waiting in the wings," Darian remarked.

- 11 -

After sliding down the mountain, the team entered some ruins that were on a small hill just above Hasty Railways. From there they looked down on Grand Central, the huge building Darian had seen the other player enter.

"I say we jump onto the train station's roof," Darian said. "Then we'll still have the high ground, and no matter which way that kid comes out, we can take him." I wanted to tell him that whoever was inside the station would be able to hear their footsteps the moment they landed, but I had said I was going to let them do this on their own, so I stayed silent.

BATTLE OF THE BOTS

"That could work," Lucas said. "But only one of us should go on the roof."

"But Wyatt say stick together, remember?" Shu said.

"Well, Wyatt's not here right now," Lucas replied, "which means *I'm* calling the shots. So with all due respect, Shu, zip it. And if you don't know what that means, ask Olivia." He laughed. "JK, Shu. Darian, I want you to go up on the roof of the train station and make as much noise as possible. Jump up and down, swing your sledgehammer around, smash things, fire your gun, whatever. Act like a total noob."

"Got it," Darian replied, his avatar already taking off at a dead run.

"What we going do?" Shu asked.

"You and I are going to sit right here," Lucas replied, "with our guns pointed straight at Darian. The minute someone makes a play for him, we open fire."

"You mean you're using Darian as bait?" Olivia asked.

"Something like that."

Just then, an alarm sounded. "Zone going shift soon," Shu said. "Train station not in next circle."

"Even better," Lucas replied. "That kid's going to come rushing out of the train station thinking he's going to score an easy kill right before he books it, but he's got another thing coming."

"Whoo-hoo! Yippee! Aye, aye, aye!"

"Darian, what the heck are you doing?" Lucas asked. "You do realize that kid can't hear you, right?"

"It helps me get into character," Darian replied as his avatar continued to leap around on the train station's roof. "Yippee-ki-yi—"

Boom!

"I'm hit!" Darian cried.

"Where'd the shot come from?" Lucas asked.

"I don't know!"

"See that dome across the plaza?" Olivia said. "I think it came from there."

"Box up, Darian," Lucas said. "And down some heals. Shu, blast that dome!"

Shu and Lucas opened fire on it, prompting whoever was inside to box up as well.

"Now advance!"

Lucas and Shu's avatars tore down the hill and then dashed up the wooden ramp that Darian had built to get onto the Grand Station's roof.

"Darian, let us into your box," Lucas said. Darian edited out a wall so they could slip inside and then closed it again.

Wyatt was impressed. Editing wasn't exactly a beginner's technique, and yet Darian had handled it with ease, which showed some real promise.

Just then their box was blasted by bullets, seemingly from all sides.

"Dig!" Lucas said. All three of them swung their sledgehammers at the roof until they broke through it and their avatars fell to the station's main floor. They stood in a circle back to back, their guns at the ready.

"What do we do now?" Darian asked. "Whoever beaned me will be waiting for us to come out."

"Or come inside, take us out," Shu said.

Another alarm sounded, indicating the zone was beginning to shift.

"We didn't see that other kid leave the station, so he's still gotta be in here somewhere," Lucas said. "Let's find him and then book it."

"But zone move soon," Shu said. "Bad for health if stay in storm. Long way to go to next circle."

"Bullets are bad for your health too, Shu," Lucas replied. "Now let's get moving."

No sooner were the words out of Lucas's mouth than the kid they were about to go hunting for jumped out of hiding. He looked like a total goofball, wearing a skin that had a loaded cheeseburger with a big tongue sticking out of it for a head, but as we were about to learn, there was nothing goofy about the way he played.

"Get him!" Lucas cried.

The three surviving members of our squad opened fire, but whether due to surprise or because their aim was so terrible, their bullets went flying in every direction but at him. Rather than firing back, the kid threw a wall up in front of him and then edited a window in the middle of it. Realizing what he was about to do, I leaned forward in my chair.

"Guys, look out! He's going to—"

Only then did I realize my mic was still muted. I scrambled to hit the unmute button, but it was too late.

The player built a cone above and below Darian, Lucas, and Shu. Then he put a wall behind them.

"Retreat!" Lucas yelled.

But the moment they tried, the player who was attacking them built a metal wall in the direction they were going, blocking their way. He had probably anticipated they would try to flee out the train station's front doors. Then he threw a brick wall up on the other side of them for good measure. In a matter of seconds, they were completely boxed in.

But that was only the beginning of their troubles.

"Shoot out the walls!" Lucas said.

In their panic, rather than all of them focusing on the same wall, which might have given at least one of them a slim chance of escaping had they gotten through it, they all shot in different directions, diluting their efforts.

That gave the kid all the time in the world to do a diagonal half-wall edit, leap up in the air, and blast them with his shotgun. Then he closed the wall so they couldn't even return fire. He did the same thing two more times, and it was all over. Their avatars collapsed, spewing their loot across the floor, and a spawn drone appeared over each body to teleport them back to Spawn Island.

"We were eliminated by UfinishedUgly?" Lucas exclaimed as the player who had just killed them ran around picking up their loot, his gamertag floating overhead. "How'd we lose to a guy with a gamertag like that?"

"Rumble Royale 101," I replied, having finally gotten my mic up and running. "He boxed you in and then took you out."

"What makes you so sure it's a *he?*" Olivia asked.

"Okay, *he, she,* or *they* boxed you in and then *he, she,* or *they* took you out. Satisfied? The point is, you're all dead."

"What could we have done to prevent the other player from boxing us in?" Darian asked.

"Lots of things," I replied. "First, you were all standing close together, which made it easy for him to trap you. So, in the future, spread out, especially if you don't know where your enemy is.

"Once you were boxed, rather than retreating—which was the worst thing you could have done, by the way, Lucas—it would have been better to focus your fire on the wall between you and the other player. The wall was made of wood, which is weak, so you would have blasted right through it and then forced him to build more walls between you. Without the element of surprise and with three players against one, he probably would have just run away."

"Or she," Olivia added.

"Or they," Lucas said, unable to resist chiming in.

Rather than taking the bait and saying something snarky in reply, I continued with my explanation.

"Box fighting is all about piece control, which means learning how to build and edit walls, ramps, cones, and stairs quickly and strategically so you can trap your opponent in your builds and they can't run away from you. If you control the builds, it's quick and easy for you to edit them and move around. Meanwhile, your opponent will be stuck having to smash through them with their sledgehammer or shoot them out, which takes longer, makes them vulnerable, and wastes their ammo.

"After UfinishedUgly boxed you in, it was like shooting fish in a barrel. Whoever they are, they must feel like a genius right now. I just hope a clip of that kill doesn't show up on TikTok or something and go viral or our streaming days will be finished before they even start. Never mind our skins; we'd have to change our gamertags as well or we'd never be able to live that down."

"Speaking of streaming," Darian said, "when do you think we'll get started with that?"

BATTLE OF THE BOTS

"Not until we're all a *lot* better than we are right now."

"Why wait?" Lucas asked, as if the answer wasn't obvious.

"Um, I don't know," I replied. "So we don't look like a bunch of total doofuses?"

"But we're called the Stream Team, remember? If we wait until we're *good enough* to start streaming, whatever that means, we'll probably never do it. Instead of hiding how terrible we are, wouldn't it be more interesting if a bunch of total noobs like us launched our stream declaring our intention to win the RRCS this year?"

"I'd watch that," Darian said.

"Me too," Shu added.

"Me three," Olivia said.

Did she have to chime in on *every* decision? She wasn't even part of the team.

"I don't know, guys," I said. "I didn't think our goal was to launch a comedy channel."

"So what if people laugh at us?" Darian replied. "It'll all be part of the fun."

"That's just the thing," I replied. "I didn't start

this squad to have fun. I started it to win."

My comment was met by dead silence. Even I was a little shocked at the coldness of my voice, but I still meant every word.

"Should we vote on it?" Lucas asked.

At that point I was tempted to tear off my headphones, throw them down on my desk in frustration, and walk away. The only thing that stopped me was knowing that Lucas was sitting right behind me, and like it or not, there was no getting away from him.

"Since when was this team a democracy?" I asked.

"It's *never* been a democracy," Lucas replied. "That's the point. I'm trying to make it one."

I couldn't help but scoff at that. Just because each team member was allowed to voice their opinion on various decisions didn't make our squad a democracy. As I was quickly learning, no matter what decision we were facing, when it came right down to it, only one vote on our team truly mattered.

And it wasn't mine.

I let out a long, loud sigh. Even though I was about to concede, I wanted to make sure it was

clear how I felt about it. "Fine, we can do it."
"Vote?" Darian asked.
"No, stream."
"All right!" he said. "Just one question . . . how?"

- 12 -

No matter what the issue was, when it came to Lucas, whenever we managed to solve one problem, he always found a way to create three more. I couldn't tell if he was doing it to be difficult or if that was just the way he was.

For instance, now that he had railroaded the rest of us into agreeing to livestream our quest to win the RRCS—or go down in flames and make utter fools of ourselves trying—we were arguing over whether we should go exclusive on one platform, such as Twitch, YouTube, or Kick, or go live on multiple platforms at once.

BATTLE OF THE BOTS

"Going live on several platforms simultaneously will give us way better exposure," Lucas insisted.

"Yeah, but it requires a huge amount of bandwidth, never mind the cycles it sucks from your CPU and GPU," I replied. "There's no sense going wide if you have to slow down your computer to do it. That would pretty much guarantee we'd lose every game."

"Oh, come on, Wyatt," Lucas said. "That machine of yours can probably livestream on a hundred platforms at once and you'd never know the difference. And you have a hardwired fiber optic Internet connection, so bandwidth isn't a problem either."

He was right, but I wasn't about to let *him* know that. A good PC could stream games at a reasonable resolution, but pretty much any big streamer had a two-PC setup, using one to stream and the other to play on, so they could stream at the highest quality without stressing their system.

"I still think it's better to go exclusive with one platform for the stream and then make clips of our best moments and turn them into YouTube Shorts, TikTok videos, and Instagram Reels to promote it," I said. "That way, we can focus all our efforts on one area rather than spreading them across multiple platforms."

In truth, I was hoping that by sticking to just one platform, we could keep a low profile until we didn't suck nearly as badly as we did at the moment.

"I agree with Wyatt," Darian said.

Finally! I thought. Someone else was chiming in, and for once they were taking my side instead of Lucas's.

"That is, I *sort of* agree with him."

Grrr . . .

"Instead of just one platform, I think we should focus on two—Twitch and Kick. Gaming is what both of those platforms are known for, so we should fish where the fish are, right? They're also the shortest path toward making money from our stream—if anyone cares about that."

"Duh. Of course we do."

Lucas again. Always about the money.

Darian was right about which platforms we should target, though. Twitch had a couple of programs that allowed streamers to make money. The lowest tier was the affiliate program, which required just fifty followers, five hundred minutes of broadcast time over seven days, and an average of at least three viewers per stream. Once we hit that level, we could split subscription revenue fifty/fifty with Twitch and accept donations from viewers. If we reached a thousand subscribers and hit a few other targets, we could become Twitch partners, which would give us an even bigger slice of the pie plus other perks.

The deal with Kick was similar. All we needed was seventy-five followers and five broadcast hours. Then we'd receive 95 percent of anything our channel earned.

Contrast those options with YouTube, which required one thousand subscribers and four thousand watch hours over the past twelve months. Unlike the subscriptions on Twitch and Kick, subs on YouTube were free, but paid or not, I had no idea how a bunch of bumbling bricks like us were going to get even one subscriber to watch our lousy channel, never mind a thousand.

"Shu, what do you think?" Darian asked.

"I fine with whatever team decide," Shu replied.

"Um . . . you're part of this team," Lucas said. "Remember?"

There was silence for a moment. Then Olivia came on. "Shu realizes that. She's just trying to be nice—unlike you, String Bean."

"Hey!"

"I have another question," I said. "Who's going to be the face of our team?"

"What do you mean?" Darian asked.

"Well, we can do the Stream Together thing on Twitch, which would show all of us on the same stream, but Kick doesn't have that option. Plus, even though my computer and Internet connection and maybe Shu's might be powerful enough to stream on multiple platforms at once, I'm not sure about you and Lucas."

"Is that your not-so-subtle way of saying *you* want to be the face of our team?" Lucas asked.

"No. I'm just saying that for practical reasons—"

"Why don't we make it a competition?" Lucas suggested.

I opened my mouth to reply, thinking he was go-

BATTLE OF THE BOTS

ing to do his usual "put it to a vote" thing, only to stop short once I realized what he had actually said.

"A competition? What do you mean?"

"To qualify to play in tournaments, each of us has to complete the Outlast 500 quest, right?" By that, he meant we each needed to play a series of battle royale games until we had outlasted a total of 500 players. Fortunately, progress toward this quest was cumulative, which meant no matter where we placed in each match—even if we were the second player killed—as long as we kept playing and surviving for as long as possible, eventually, we would all outlast a total of 500 enemy players. It was simple enough to do, but it could take a while, depending on a player's skills.

"Yeah. I completed that quest years ago," I said.

"Well, the rest of us haven't," Lucas replied, "and seeing as we're launching a new team, I think you should create a new account and redo it."

"What?"

"Each game consists of 100 players, so we'll each have to play at least five games to qualify, right?"

I had to laugh at that. "Yeah, if you *win* all five

games, but from what I've seen so far—"

"We should do it as solos too rather than as a squad," Lucas continued, barreling forward as if I hadn't spoken. "That way, we'll each rank up faster. Now, here's where the competition part comes in. Whenever we play, each of us should stream on Twitch or Kick or whatever platform we choose. Once we all complete the quest, whoever's stream is the most popular will become our team's official channel."

I took a second to consider Lucas's proposal before responding. It wasn't a bad idea. Seeing as Lucas had virtually no profile as a gamer, that put us on an even playing field—except for the fact that I was a far better player than him, which would make my stream *way* more entertaining.

Then again, Lucas was no dummy, so if he was pushing this idea, he probably figured he had some kind of edge. But even if he did, he had such a repellant personality that I was still confident I could get more viewers than him no matter what sort of tricks he pulled. His computer was also such a pile of junk that the moment he tried to play *and* stream at the same time, I figured it would probably explode.

"Works for me," I said, barely able to contain a smile at how easy this would be. "How about the rest of you?"

"Sounds like fun!" Darian said, as positive as ever.

"I like too," Shu added.

"What about you, Olivia?" Lucas asked.

"What?" I exclaimed. "She's not even part of—"

"I love it!" Olivia said. "And may the best woman win!"

- 13 -

As it turns out, I probably should have listened to Olivia—and I definitely shouldn't have listened to Lucas.

For starters, the whole point of pulling the Stream Team together was to create a unified squad, just like a group of real-life soldiers, people who could rely on one another and who had each other's backs. Instead, Lucas's idea pitted us against each other right from the get-go. I realized it was just a friendly competition, but it was still a popularity contest, and there was no way I was going to lose—especially to Lucas. I'm sure he felt the same way about me. I wasn't sure what the long-term consequences would be for the team if either of us won, but we'd have to sort that out later.

After doing some research on what made for a popular video game stream, I put some of the ideas I found into practice. That began with streaming at a set time each day when most people would be online, which turned out to be from 7:00 to 10:00 p.m.

Following another tip, an hour or so before I started streaming, I dropped into some other streams and hinted that I had a stream coming up as well. That got me banned from a few streams at first, seeing as no one likes a self-promoter, but I learned my lesson and took a subtler approach after that, which didn't get me banned at least, although I had no idea how effective it was. After all, who would want to watch a nobody like me when so many other big-name players were out there?

I considered promoting my stream on my social media channels as well, but that would have meant tipping off the kids at school about what I was up to, and I still wasn't ready to do that—not until we were much, *much* better.

KEVIN MILLER

When it came to the stream itself, I tried to imitate some of my favorite gamers and be as engaging as possible—talking constantly and expressing as much emotion as I was able whenever I killed someone or whenever I got killed, trash talking the other players at every opportunity, whether they were better than me or worse. But as I soon realized, while famous streamers had big personalities and hundreds of commenters to respond to, which kept the conversation flowing, I was an introvert, which made talking difficult at the best of times. It felt like what few words I was able to get out just disappeared into the ether, and I had no idea who—if anyone—was watching or listening.

I didn't have to wait long for an answer to that question. That's because the evidence was right there on the screen: zero. Night after night, that's how it was—zero viewers, zero comments, and zero interest. I wasn't surprised, but it was still depressing.

"So, how's everyone's stream going?" I asked as the members of the team gathered in the school cafeteria after I had spent yet another disappointing night of broadcasting into the void. We'd all

BATTLE OF THE BOTS

agreed not to watch each other's streams until we had each completed the quest, just to keep the results a surprise. However, my experience was so grim that even if I had been tempted to peek at anyone else's stream, I wouldn't have done it, just in case they were doing better than me.

"Great!" Lucas said. "I completed the quest last night—correction. Early this morning—and at its peak, my stream had over one hundred viewers."

"One hundred?" I didn't think my eyes could have opened any wider until Darian piped up.

"Wow, and here I thought I was doing well with twenty-five viewers. But I completed the quest too, and guess what? I got two subscribers!"

"You got . . . subscribers?" I asked, slack-jawed.

"Yeah!" Darian replied. "Well, two friends used their free Amazon subs to subscribe to my stream, but a sub's a sub, right?"

"You got it," Lucas said as the two of them high-fived. "Ka-ching! Isn't that right, Shu?"

Shu high-fived Lucas with one hand as she poured hot water into a bowl of instant ramen noodles with the other. As I stared at the noodles floating in the water, my mind churned with a mixture of jealousy and despair. Surely at least Shu was doing poorer than me, although I didn't know what could be worse than zero, except maybe getting banned from the platform altogether. But there was no way that would happen to someone like Shu.

"How about you, Shu?" I asked, speaking slowly not only so she would be sure to understand me but also because I was afraid to hear the answer. "How's your stream going?"

BATTLE OF THE BOTS

"Five hundred viewers. Can you believe that?" Lucas said, jumping in before Shu could reply. When I turned to her for confirmation, she smiled and nodded as she stirred her noodles.

"Five hundred?" I asked. "How?"

"Would you believe Shu is a bit of a celebrity back home?" Darian said.

"She's a . . . a what?" I asked. I'd heard the term "flabbergasted" before, but that was the first time I knew what it felt like.

"Well, a small 'c' celebrity, right?" Darian said. When Shu frowned in confusion, he switched to Mandarin to explain what he meant. Then she smiled and nodded.

"Singer," she said, pointing to herself. "Win big competition on TV."

"She was on a Chinese knock-off of American Idol," Darian explained. "You know, one of those singing shows where everyone competes to be the next big pop star. She didn't win the whole thing, but she did represent the entire region of Hong Kong, which has a population of over seven million people. So, all she had to do was put the word out to her fans and, voila! Suddenly people were flocking online to watch her play."

"You're . . . a singer?" I said, so shocked that I was still only able to get a few words out at a time. "On TV?"

She nodded again, then launched into a pitch-perfect version of Rihanna's "Umbrella"—in perfect English, no less, with no trace of her Chinese accent. The other students sitting nearby stopped and stared, then applauded when she finished. She smiled and waved, her face reddening in response to all the attention.

I closed my eyes and shook my head before opening them again. This was all too much. "But your accent. How . . . ?"

"She learned the song phonetically," Darian explained. "She just learned the sounds of each word. She had no idea what the song was about until I explained it to her the other day. Isn't that hilarious?"

"Yeah, really funny," I said as a sick feeling formed deep in the pit of my stomach.

"How about your stream, Wyatt?" Darian asked. "You have so much experience as a gamer, you must be killing it."

"Yeah, Wyatt, how *is* your stream going?" Lucas asked before he took a big bite of a bologna and mustard sandwich on white bread. Judging from the glint in his eye, I had a feeling he already knew the answer.

Not wanting to admit what an abysmal failure my own streaming efforts had been, all I could do was stare down at the table in despair, my eyes stinging with tears. It was the closest I'd been to crying since I was a little kid.

Just when I was thinking about making a run for it, I heard the last thing I was expecting—laughter.

I looked up to find the other three members of the Stream Team grinning at me.

"Got ya!" Lucas said, slapping me on the back so hard that I could practically feel his fingerprints embedding themselves into my back.

"What?" I said, looking from face to face in confusion.

- 14 -

My eyes must have been redder than I realized because when Darian looked at me, his smile faded, and his face softened with concern.

"Oh, Wyatt, we were just joking. Lucas, I told you we shouldn't have pushed things so far."

"Ah, he's tough," Lucas said, slapping me on the back again, which caused me to flinch in pain. "He can take it."

"Ow!" I cried, rubbing my shoulder. "Would you cut that out?"

"Sorry," Lucas said, taking another bite of his sandwich and offering a sheepish smile.

BATTLE OF THE BOTS

"Wait a second," I said, my despair replaced by a flicker of anger. "You mean you guys weren't serious?"

I turned to Shu, whose face was glowing with embarrassment, and she shook her head, her mouth too full of noodles to speak.

"We—that is, Lucas—thought it would be funny if we all pretended our streams were a huge success and yours was, well, what it is," Darian said.

"You guys watched my stream?" I asked.

"Of course!" Lucas said. "I watched everyone's.

We all did."

"But we had a deal!"

"Actually," Lucas said, holding up his index finger, "I'd say it was more of a gentleman's agreement—or gentlewoman's," he added with a nod to Shu.

"So, your streams are doing as badly as mine?" I asked, more relieved than angry now.

"Technically, no," Lucas replied, "but practically, yes."

I frowned at him and then shook my head. "What the heck is that supposed to mean?"

"I created a few Twitch accounts and then had some of my Warhammer buddies log into them while I was streaming," Lucas explained. "So, *technically*, I had a few viewers, but in reality, no one was watching—not even my friends, as far as I can tell. At least, none of them commented. They all think Rumble Royale is a little kid's game, by the way."

"Why am I not surprised? And you other two—you didn't have any viewers either?" I asked, turning to Darian and Shu.

"I wasn't lying about the subs," Darian said. "A couple of friends from the Medi-Taters subscribed to my stream, and I think one of them even watched it for a few seconds, but that's it."

"What about you, Shu?" I asked. "Are you really a famous pop singer with millions of fans in Hong Kong, or was that a lie too?"

Shu smiled and shook her head. "TV show real but never made it past audition."

"Really?" I replied. "With that voice?"

She shrugged. "Lots of people in China. Many good singers."

"Huh," I said, still processing what felt like a near-death experience. "So, we all suck then. We're a bunch of total bots."

"Maybe *that's* what we should call our squad," Darian said. "Total Bots."

"No way," Lucas replied, shaking his head. "Sounds too much like a self-fulfilling prophecy. If we don't start *thinking* like winners, we'll never *be* winners. Isn't that what all your mindfulness gobbledygook is all about, Darian?"

"Not exactly, but—"

"Did all of you at least complete your quests?" I asked, cutting Darian off. I had completed my quest the first night, but I had kept streaming for a few more nights anyway, knowing it would probably take the other members of the Stream Team a bit longer. Besides, I thought it would give me a chance to build a bigger audience, even though that didn't exactly pan out.

They all nodded in unison.

"Well, we accomplished that much at least," I said. "Now we can start competing in cash cups. But we still need to answer an important question."

"Oh, yeah? What's that?" Lucas asked after he stuck a straw into a juice box and took a long pull from it.

"Who's going to be the face of our team?"

I waited for someone to respond, but all they did was give each other a questioning look as if they didn't know what I was talking about, so I decided to clarify. "What I mean is, seeing as the streaming thing didn't exactly help us pick a winner, should we vote on it instead?"

Lucas finished draining his juice box and then took aim at a nearby recycling bin as if he were shooting a free throw. "We already did," he said as he took the shot. It hit the rim, teetered on the edge for a moment, and then bounced onto the floor. As he leaped up to grab his juice box before he got in trouble with the lunchroom monitor, I felt that flicker of anger return. First the practical joke, and now they were voting without me too? It felt like I was facing a full-on mutiny, and I knew exactly who was leading it.

"Wait a second," I said, my anger bubbling into a roar. "You took a vote without even telling me? Are you forgetting who pulled this team together? Who taught you how to play the game? Who showed you how to—"

"We didn't forget any of that," Darian said as Lucas returned to his seat.

"As for the vote," Lucas added, "there was no reason to include you because the verdict was unanimous. Isn't that right?" He looked at the other two for confirmation and received nods in response.

All I could do was stare at Lucas, flabbergasted yet again.

"So that's it, then? I don't even get a say in what happens to my own team?"

"Nope," Lucas replied, crossing his arms and grinning. I couldn't believe the audacity of this guy!

"Oh, Lucas, quit giving him such a hard time," Darian said. "There's no need for you to vote, Wyatt, because we all voted for the same person—you."

"You did?" I said, afraid I was going to get whiplash from all the sudden mood changes.

"Of course," Darian replied. "Not only are you the most experienced, you're also the most entertaining."

I arched an eyebrow in surprise. "I am?"

Shu grinned and nodded. "Very funny."

"Well, technically, it's more of a laughing *at* you than a laughing *with* you situation," Lucas said, "but still . . ."

"Lucas . . ." Darian said, drawing out his name in warning. But at that point I was too relieved to worry about anyone making fun of me, least of all Lucas.

"You really think I'm good at it?" I asked, trying not to make it sound like I was fishing for compliments, even though I really needed one about then.

"Not that we want you to get a big head or anything . . ." Lucas muttered.

"Yes, we do," Darian said. "That is, no, we don't want you to get a swelled head, but we do think you're good at it. I had no idea what to talk about while I was streaming, but you seemed to have no problem. And your trash talk? Man, I think we could all take some lessons. Even Lucas."

The greasy-haired genius offered up a mock frown in response. "Hey, I 'resemble' that remark!"

Just then, the warning bell rang, signaling that lunch was about to end. We all stood up and gathered our things.

"Now that that's all sorted out," I said, "I guess there's just one thing left for us to do."

"That's right," Darian said. "Enter our first cash cup!"

"Ka-ching!" Lucas added, reaching out to give Shu a high five. But when she tried to return the gesture, her physics textbook slipped out from under her arm and landed right on top of Lucas's foot, corner first.

He yelped in pain, jumping up and down while clutching his injured foot.

"More like ka-ch*ow*," I muttered.

Lucas stopped hopping and fixed me with a glare. "Hey, don't you know it's rude to laugh at other people's misery?"

"Well, technically, it's more of a laughing *with* you than a laughing *at* you situation," I said, struggling to stifle a grin, "but still . . ."

"We'll see who's laughing when I get my hands on you!" Lucas said as he released his foot and chased me out of the cafeteria, Darian and Shu right behind him.

And if I didn't know better, I could have sworn Lucas was smiling.

I know I certainly was.

- 15 -

I could give you a blow-by-blow account of our first tournament together as a squad, detailing the dizzying ups and the disheartening downs of our initial attempt to cash in on the *Rumble Royale* gold mine. But I thought it might be better if I left that job to someone else: our "fans."

Fans, you say? Considering how terrible our first efforts at streaming had gone, you're probably wondering how we could have had even one fan, never mind several. In case you missed it, that's why I wrote it as "fans," not *fans*. The quotation marks are supposed to make it sound ironic. But before I turn things over to them, I should provide a bit of background.

Like so many other life-changing events, it started with an accident. Seconds after landing on what I thought would be a safe, out-of-the way spot on the map where we could stock up on supplies without anyone bothering us, we got into a firefight with another team who tried to ambush us—definitely not part of the plan.

However, by some miracle, I managed to kill one of them, and then the rest of their squad took off.

When the dead player's gamertag showed up in my kill feed, I thought I recognized it from somewhere, so I did a quick online search. That's when I realized we might have hit the jackpot.

"Hey, guys, that player I just killed? He's kind of famous!"

"Really?" Darian said. "Cool!"

"Yeah, he's part of a pro team. I just looked him up on the Rumble Royale leaderboard, and he's number seven hundred and fifty in the rankings."

Lucas scoffed. "Seven hundred and fifty? Doesn't sound too impressive to me."

BATTLE OF THE BOTS

"Well, that's out of over 11.5 million players, which puts him in the top 0.1 percent," I replied. "And he's earned just over twenty thousand dollars so far."

"Twenty thousand dollars?" Darian said. "Wow! I can't believe you killed him, Wyatt. Way to go!"

"I can't either. But we'd better watch it. His teammates are going to be ticked. In fact, I wouldn't be surprised if they come back and—"

Just then an alert sounded, and the words *Bounty Started: You're Being Targeted* appeared on my screen.

"Uh-oh," I said.

"What wrong?" Shu asked.

"Someone just took out a bounty on me."

"Really? Do you think it's one of the dead guy's teammates?" Darian asked.

"I doubt it," I said. "Bounties are assigned randomly, but you never know."

"So, what does it mean?" Lucas asked.

"It means whoever took out the bounty has six minutes to find me and kill me. If they do, they win seventy-five gold bars."

I glanced at the Threat Monitor on the top-right corner of my screen. It featured a timer that was already counting down from six minutes and a type of radar that gave me a rough idea of how close my pursuer was. So far there was only one yellow bar, which meant I was safe. If it went to two yellow bars, I would have to get moving. Three red bars would mean the hunter was nearly on top of me.

"And if you kill them?" Lucas asked.

"*I* get the seventy-five gold bars. But I don't have to kill them to get the gold. I just have to avoid dying."

"What's the gamertag for the player you killed?" Lucas asked. As soon as I told him, I heard him typing in the background. His mom had worked things out with their neighbor, so he was back at home, leaching off their Wi-Fi again.

"What are you doing?" I asked.

"Seeing if he's streaming the tournament."

Inspired by my gaming setup, Lucas had made a return trip to the dump and charmed the woman at the gate into letting him dig through a pallet of monitors. He managed to find one that worked, so now he had two monitors running, one for gaming and the other for everything else. I couldn't believe his computer was still running at all, never mind being able to support two screens at once.

"What for?" I asked.

"Just give me a minute."

As he continued to type, another alert sounded.

"We should really get moving, Lucas," I said. "The zone's going to shift soon. The rest of you, keep looting."

"Found it!" Lucas said, followed by more typing.

"Um, Lucas, in case you forgot, we're in the middle of our first tournament here. That other team could come back at any moment and—"

"I know, I know."

Just then, a second yellow bar appeared on my Threat Monitor. I scanned the area to see if I could spot anyone trying to sneak up on us, but the terrain was so steep that it blocked my view.

"All right, well, I don't know about the rest of you, but I'm out of here," I said, marking a spot on the map that was just inside where the next circle would appear. "Let's all head here."

"Done!" Lucas said as his avatar finally started moving again, and he and the others bounded along beside me.

"What were you doing?" Darian asked.

"Just engaging in a bit of trash talk," Lucas said.

"On the dead player's stream?"

Lucas laughed. "Where else?"

Somehow I had a feeling we were all going to regret that.

"What you say to him?" Shu asked.

"I just told them that he and his teammates were a bunch of scrubs, and if they think they can take out a bounty on one of my friends and get away with it, they've got another thing coming."

"But we don't even know if they're the ones who took out the bounty," I reminded him.

"Plus, it sounds like these guys are pretty good," Darian added. "I'm not sure if provoking them is the best idea."

"Um, I hate to break it to you," Olivia said—somehow she always found a way into our games, even though I kept telling her to back off and let Shu play on her own—"but I just looked them up, and those *guys* are actually *girls*. Which means you *definitely* shouldn't have provoked them."

"Well, girls or not, I also might have mentioned the name of our squad—and the link to our stream—and said if anyone was interested in seeing how a *real* squad played, they should drop in for a peek."

"You did what?" I cried, shifting my attention to my second monitor, which featured our stream. I hadn't bothered looking at it so far, seeing as I assumed no one was watching us. But when I glanced at the view counter, my eyeballs nearly popped out.

"A hundred viewers!"

"We've got fans!" Darian said.

"And look—they're writing comments!" Olivia added.

Fans? Comments? This just keeps getting better, I thought—until I started reading those comments. Most of them were so nasty that I can't repeat them here, but below is a brief sample of the tamer ones, just to give you an idea.

Squidslap: Dude, you know that having a brain can cause brain cancer, right? No danger here tho

PikiPokiHype: U want some marshmallows to go with all that campin?

RaginHippie: Return the skin!

Babydaisy: Y'all aim like a drunk stormtrooper on a roller coaster

SlimInnit: Uninstall IRL

StormCruz: Man my IQ goin' down just watchin u

Wokwithchan: Yo, I bet u gotta face that looks like I drew it with my left hand

Stopthehumanity: Is it cold and lonely down there in your mom's basement?

SnipeSnap: I hope you and your team get carried away by ants

Kidwiththegoldengums: If they put your brain in a bird, it'd fly backward

BananaSpit: Factory reset ASAP lol

PatientHero: Did your goldfish just flop all over the controller or sumpin?

Funkypuzzler: Bruh, my dog has more skills in his tail than you have on your entire team

Midway through reading them, I also realized something else. In addition to watching us play,

BATTLE OF THE BOTS

anyone tuning in to our stream could also hear everything we said, as became clear when they started commenting on that in real time too.

XstreamGene: We not ur fans, dude. We the griefers yo mama warned u bout
TotalRecalled: Noob can't tell the difference between a comment and a roast
Showdownz: Stream Team? More like Tick Tock Bots
BerryBro: Odd Squad
ChemicalSmothers: Bot Bros
SnoopDonkey: The NPC Three
HardReset: There's four of 'em
SnoopDonkey: Not 4 long
HardReset: lol

See what I mean? "Fans."

As the insults continued to scroll down the screen, I realized I had to do something to stop the bleeding, and fast.

"Mute your mics," I said. "Radio silence from here on out. Text only!"

- 16 -

"Look on the bright side," Darian said the following day at school as he, Shu, and I debriefed in the cafeteria. "At least now people know who we are."

"Hey, look, it's the Scream Team!" someone called out.

"No, it's the Beam Team," someone else said.

"The Dream Team," another person said. "As in, 'dream on'!"

So much for keeping our quest for *Rumble Royale* glory a secret from the kids at school.

Surprisingly, we didn't do too badly in the tournament, placing in the top ten. But one of our

BATTLE OF THE BOTS

"fans" cut together a clip of our deaths that went viral—all of us killed by the pro team Lucas had insulted—and it seemed like half the kids in school had watched it.

It wasn't how I had hoped things would go, but seeing as the Stream Team was now on the map, there was no way we could back out—at least, I hoped no one wanted to back out.

"Where Lucas?" Shu asked, looking around the cafeteria for him.

"I don't know," I replied, checking my watch. "He was supposed to meet us here fifteen minutes ago."

As if he'd heard us talking about him, at that very moment, Lucas ambled into the cafeteria, looking more disheveled than ever. He seemed to be in a total daze, his eyes wandering around the room as if he'd forgotten where he was or how he got there.

"Yo, Lucas, over here!" Darian called out, waving to him.

Changing his direction slightly, Lucas wandered over to our table and plunked down in a chair, his eyes fixed on the floor.

KEVIN MILLER

"Hey, Lucas, what's wrong?" Darian said. "You look like you haven't slept a wink."

Lucas raised his head and met Darian's gaze. "That's probably because I haven't."

Darian laughed, trying to make light of it. "Hey, it was only one loss, and check it out. We're famous now!"

Rather than offering a sarcastic reply, as was his habit, Lucas merely lowered his eyes to the floor once again.

"Lucas, is something wrong?" I asked, a surge of concern growing in my chest. When Lucas raised his head again, I was shocked to see tears glistening in his eyes.

"It's my older brother," he said. "We got into a terrible fight, and he . . . he smashed my computer. I was so scared I ran away from home."

Continue the story with book 3!

Made in the USA
Las Vegas, NV
03 September 2024

94709216R00075